Grass Sandals

Grass Sandals

The Travels of Basho

by

DAWNINE SPIVAK

illustrated by DEMI

Atheneum Books for Young Readers

Atheneum Books for Young Readers
An imprint of Simon & Schuster Children's Publishing Division
1230 Avenue of the Americas
New York, New York 10020

Book design by Becky Terhune
The text of this book is set in Bernhard Modern.
The illustrations are rendered in colored ink using Oriental brushes.

First Edition
Printed in Hong Kong by South China Printing Co. (1988) Ltd.
10 9 8 7 6 5 4 3 2 1

Library of Congress Cataloging-in-Publication Data
Spivak, Dawnine.
Grass sandals : the travels of Basho / by Dawnine Spivak ;
illustrated by Demi.
p. cm.
Summary: A simple retelling of the travels of seventeenth-century
Japanese poet, Basho, across his island homeland. Includes examples of
the haiku verses he composed.
ISBN 0-689-80776-7
1. Matsuo, Basho, 1644–1694 Oku no hosomichi—Juvenile literature.
2. Matsuo, Basho, 1644–1694—Journeys—Japan—Juvenile literature.
3. Japan—Description and travel—Juvenile literature. 4. Matsuo,
Basho, 1644–1694—Adaptations—Juvenile literature. 5. Haiku—
Translations into English—Juvenile literature. [1. Matsuo, Basho,
1644–1694. 2. Poets, Japanese. 3. Japan—Description and travel.
4. Haiku.] I. Demi, ill. II. Title.
PL794.4Z50487   1997
895.6'132—dc20
95-46705

For Sam Yamashita, who gave me the gift of Japanese
literature, and for my sixteen-year-old daughter, Asha,
who said, "Mom, nothing happens in this book"—
which is what Westerners say about Japanese writing.
—D. S.

For children of all ages
—Demi

Traditionally, poems in the form called haiku are characterized
by seventeen syllables broken into three lines with five, seven,
and five syllables respectively. Each haiku includes language that
appeals to two of the five senses—sight, hearing, smell, touch,
and taste, or the additional sense of movement.

The characters of Japanese writing, the kanji, often follow the
forms of nature. In this book, for example, the character for
mountain can be seen to resemble the shape of a mountain, *rain*
looks like rain, *river* a river, and so forth.

Grass Sandals

There were old men of China who made themselves
nests in trees and lived in the branches.

YAMA

mountain

alone in my house—
only the morning glories
straggle to my door

But let me tell you the story of Basho, who lived in Japan and walked all over his island country writing poems.

Three hundred years ago, he lived in a small house next to a river. A friend gave him a basho, or banana tree. He planted it near his house and liked this tree with ragged leaves so much that he changed his name to Basho.

Basho would sit in the doorway of his small house, sit with his breakfast bowl, look out at the river and mountains, and pour his tea in the company of morning glories.

But one spring day, Basho felt restless and decided to travel. He decided to walk across Japan. He didn't need much—a rainhat made of tree bark, a raincoat made of thick grass to protect his black robe. He prepared for his journey by sewing his torn pants and stitching a string on his hat so that it wouldn't fly off in the wind.

suddenly it pours—
shivering little monkey
needs a grass raincoat

雨

AME

rain

To his hat, he said: "Hat, I will soon show you cherry blossoms."

And he scribbled on his hat: Soon, cherry blossoms. Basho closed his small house and walked to the river.

Basho began his journey on a boat, and many of his friends kept him company for a few miles on the river. His friends brought him presents for his trip: a paper coat to keep off chills, writing paper, an ink stone, and for his feet on their long walk, woven grass sandals. So little was needed for simple traveling. He carried it all with him tied up in a cloth.

川

KAWA
river

one morning at dawn
I wade in the wide river—
pants wet to my knees

When they had crossed the river, Basho climbed out of the boat and waved to his friends. On the shore was a waterfall. He ducked into a cave behind the streaming water and laughed as it sprinkled his face.

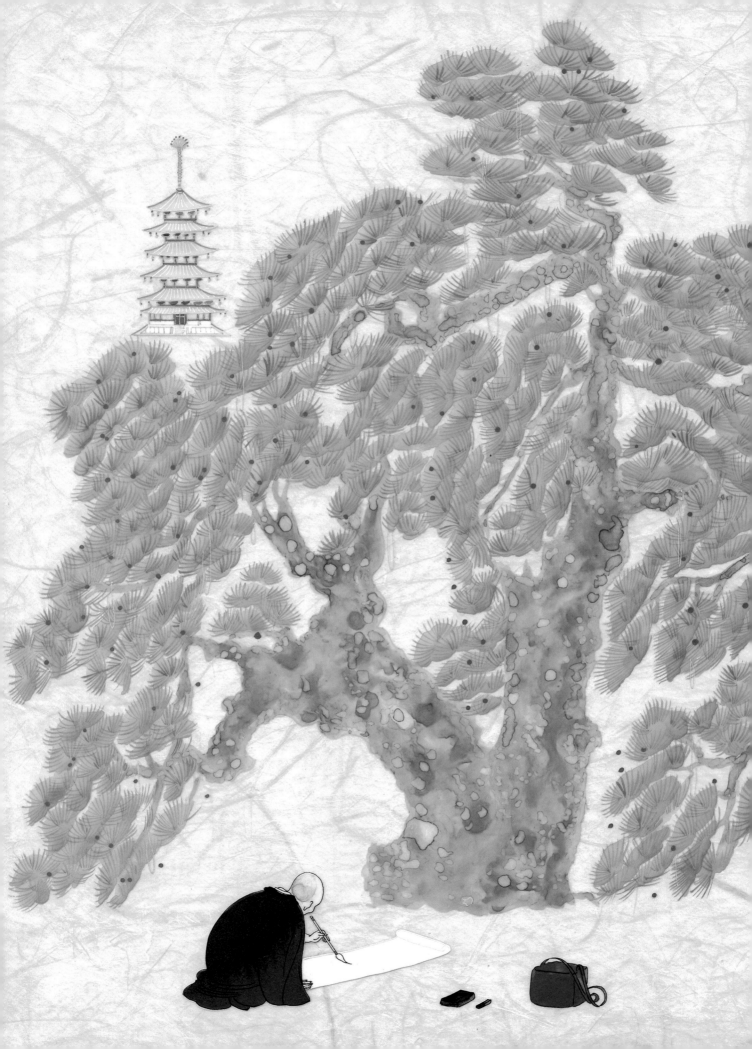

木

KI

tree

I walk to find you
sometimes five or six miles—
cherries in blossom

In his grass sandals and black robe, Basho walked and walked—looking like a black crow, he thought. Near an old temple he found a twin pine tree one thousand years old.

Basho sat and wrote a poem to this ancient, twisted tree.

Picking up his pack and climbing the winding paths, he was surprised by satiny red bark in a spring orchard, and to these trees, too, he chanted a poem.

For finally, he had kept his promise to his hat. He walked beneath the cherry trees in blossom and under the flowering branches met an old friend whose hair was as white as the petals.

At night he often rested his head on grass pillows. Sometimes he slept on flowers, in huts, or in paper rooms. Sometimes he rested in a horse stall or in a bed where fleas nipped him. He slept in fishing villages and smelled the fishy smells.

a tiny pink crab
tickling me climbs up my leg
from glistening sea

UO
fish

Basho took his baths in hot springs, splashed in cold streams, and swam in the sea.

He ate whatever he found or was given along the way: A farmer gave him a cucumber or a radish, an old woman invited him to share her noodles.

Some days he made a fire, put water in a pot, and cooked rice and beans for his supper. Then he rolled the leftovers into rice balls to eat the next day as he journeyed.

火

HI

fire

let's peel cucumbers
pick up fallen red apples
for our small supper

馬

UMA
horse

Once a trusting farmer lent him a horse to ride across a
wide, grassy field. The wind blew on Basho's suntanned
face as the horse trotted through the clover.

hibiscus flowers
munched up in the horse's mouth
eaten one by one

When he heard a grasshopper or saw the horse eating flowers or spied a hawk circling, he took his ink brush and wrote a quick poem. Basho sent the horse back to the farmer with a poem in a pouch tied to the saddle.

In a mountain village, Basho met friends and they had a party to watch the full moon. Drinking tea and rice wine, each could find a small moon reflected in the bottom of his cup. While clouds and stars and shadows lifted, they created poems together, sitting under the night sky.

winking in the night
through holes in my paper wall—
moon and Milky Way
(Issa)

月

TSUKI

moon

友
TOMO
friend

The next morning as Basho was leaving, one friend gave him new grass sandals with laces dyed blue like the iris.

"Good-bye, my friend, and thank you, thank you."

Basho hugged his friend. Crisscrossing the blue ties of his sandals around his ankles, he set out again on his walk across his island country of Japan.

stems of new iris
blooming right on my own feet—
shoelaces dyed blue

界

KAI
world

His blue-laced sandals carried him to distant beaches and fields and forests. Basho stopped to write a poem when he found a creature or person or plant that opened his eyes and his heart. He watched the fog curve over the hills. He noticed a cricket. Sleeping in a leaky hut, he smelled the rain. Each morning he tasted his tea.

In the evening he heard a frog leap into a pond. And so, three hundred years ago he traveled, and the world was his home.

old and quiet pond
suddenly a frog plops in—
a deep water sound

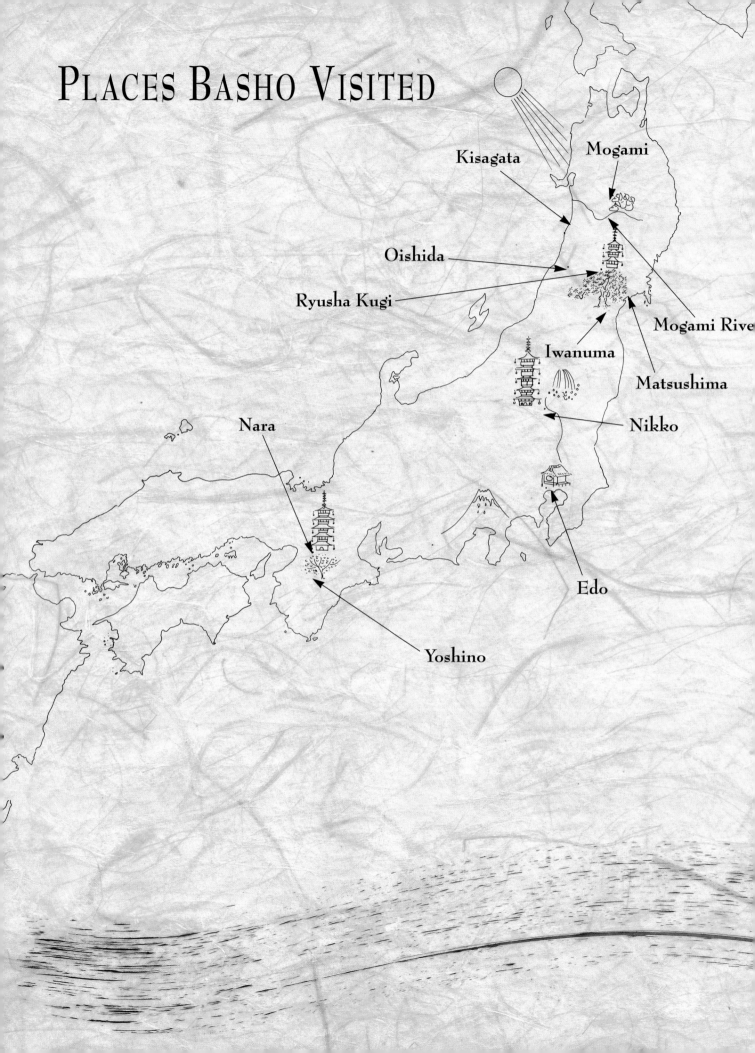

Places Basho Visited

Kisagata

Mogami

Oishida

Ryusha Kugi

Mogami River

Iwanuma

Matsushima

Nikko

Nara

Edo

Yoshino

WHAT BASHO SAW

Matsuo Basho, the haiku poet most loved and honored in his country, lived in seventeenth-century Japan (1644–1694).

He wrote journals of his travels in *haibun*, a diary of prose and poems. The places that he loved—the shrines and mountains and villages—can still be visited, and the poems remain as fresh as new leaves.

The journey of *Grass Sandals* compresses and combines events from several of Basho's travels.

At the age of fifty, Basho sold his small house in Edo and set out on his last journey.

The haiku on the page with the Japanese character Tsuki (moon) was created by Issa, another Japanese poet who lived a century after Basho.

山鳥や揺りおこす

ほの梅

鶯や柳

武陵芭蕉

鶯や柳

梅の花